THE CONSEQUENCES OF HEART'S CHOICE

AADISH JAIN

Made with ♥ on the Notion Press Platform
www.notionpress.com

"To the power of love and the beauty of heartbreak, this book is dedicated to the two musketeers who changed my life forever."

Contents

Acknowledgements *vii*

1. Chapter 1 1
2. Chapter 2 4
3. Chapter 3 8
4. Chapter 4 10
5. Chapter 5 12
6. Chapter 6 15
7. Chapter 7 18
8. Chapter 8 20
9. Chapter 9 22
10. Chapter 10 24
11. Chapter 11 28
12. Chapter 12 30
13. Chapter 13 33
14. Chapter 14 35
15. Chapter 15 39
16. Chapter 16 44
17. Chapter 17 48

About The Author 55

Acknowledgements

Dear Readers,

I want to express my sincerest gratitude to all who have made this book possible. Writing a book is a long and challenging journey, and I am grateful for all the support and encouragement I have received along the way.

First and foremost, I would like to thank my family and friends, who have always provided support and motivation whenever I needed it. Your love and encouragement have been the driving force behind this book, and I am forever grateful.

I also want to extend my appreciation to my editor and publisher, who helped me refine my writing and bring my vision to life. Your guidance and expertise have been invaluable, and I am so grateful to have had the opportunity to work with you.

A special thank you to all the readers who have taken the time to read this book. Your support and feedback mean the world to me, and I am so grateful for the opportunity to share my story with you.

Last but not least, I would like to thank the universe for all the opportunities and experiences that have shaped my life and inspired me to write this book. I am truly grateful for the journey, and this book will touch your heart and inspire you in your own life.

With love and gratitude,

Aadish Jain

CHAPTER ONE

Aadish was well-known among his peers and teachers for his kindness and helpful nature. His friends often sought his advice and guidance, as he was known for his level-headedness and problem-solving skills. Aadish was a keen learner and loved exploring new subjects and expanding his knowledge. He was also an avid sportsman who enjoyed playing Chess and Basketball in his free time.

Aadish was close to his family, especially his parents, who were proud of their son's achievements and hard work. They often encouraged him to chase his dreams and gave him the support he needed to excel in his studies.

In his free time, Aadish loved to spend time with his friends and family, going for picnics and trying out new restaurants. He also had a keen interest in music and loved playing the guitar in his leisure time. Despite his busy schedule, Aadish made time for what he loved and enjoyed a well-rounded lifestyle.

Aadish was a well-rounded individual who was respected and loved by those who knew him. His hard work, determination, kindness and compassion made him an inspiration to those around him.

Anjali had always wanted to become a doctor and help people in need. Her passion for academics and assisting others to fueled her drive to succeed in the National Eligibility cum Entrance Test (NEET). She would spend long hours every day studying and revising her lessons. Her shy and reserved nature often isolated her from her peers, but she was always focused on becoming a doctor. Despite her struggles, Anjali never lost sight of her ambition and worked hard to achieve it. Her dedication to her studies was admired by those who knew her, and she was widely regarded as a gifted student. Anjali's unwavering commitment to her goal inspired others, and her journey to becoming a doctor was a testament to her resilience and determination.

Their mutual friend, Kashravi, was a close bond between Aadish and Anjali. They had known each other for many years and had a lot of mutual interests and values. Kashravi was always there to support both of them in their ups and downs and was known for bringing people together. Aadish and Anjali often talked about how much they appreciated Kashravi's friendship and how grateful they were to have someone like her. Even miles apart, they always connected through phone calls, text messages, and video calls. Kashravi was the glue that held their friendship together, and they both valued their relationship with him deeply.

Shubhi was Aadish's best friend. She had known him since they were kids, and they shared an unbreakable bond. Shubhi was a cheerful girl who loved to make people smile, and she was always there for Aadish when he needed a shoulder to lean on.

The story begins in December when Anjali approaches Aadish for help with her studies. Little did he know, this was just the start of a journey that would change his life forever.

Aadish and Anjali met through a mutual friend and soon became close. Aadish started helping Anjali with her studies, specifically in physics and chemistry, as he was well-versed in those subjects.

CHAPTER TWO

It had been almost a year since Aadish and Anjali first met through their mutual friend. They had grown close, spending countless hours talking about everything under the sun.

From their dreams and aspirations to their fears and insecurities, they shared a bond that was unlike any other.

Anjali had always known that she was in love with Aadish. But she was scared of ruining their friendship by confessing her feelings. She had seen it happen so many times before, where a confession of love turned into a broken company.

But, as time passed, she realized that she couldn't hide her feelings.

It was a typical December evening, and Aadish was helping Anjali with her studies as she was preparing for her NEET exams, and he was preparing for his JEE exams.

They had been video calling for their study sessions, and on this particular day, Anjali had something on her mind. After their video call ended, Anjali mustered up the courage to confess her love to Aadish. She had planned it all out, and as soon as they finished the chapter, she took a deep breath and blurted it out.

"Aadish, I have something to tell you. I'm in love with you."

Aadish was taken aback by Anjali's confession. He had never thought of her that way, and he was shocked. He had always considered her one of his closest friends, and he didn't want to jeopardize their friendship by getting into a romantic relationship.

"Anjali, I don't know what to say,

I had no idea that you felt this way.

Can we talk about this later?

I need some time to think about my feelings," Aadish replied. trying to buy himself some time to process what was happening.

Anjali was disappointed by Aadish's response, but she understood. She knew this was a big decision for both of them, and she didn't want to pressure him into anything. So, she agreed to give him some time to think about it.

Just as he tried to come to terms with Anjali's confession, Shubhi, his best friend, also revealed her feelings for him. Aadish was now in a dilemma; on the one hand was the girl he had known for a long time, and on the other was the girl he considered his closest friend.

Aadish sought Shubhi's advice, and she encouraged him to follow his heart and choose the girl he truly loved.

Aadish was in a fix. He had never imagined being caught in a love triangle between two of the most influential people in his life - his best friend, Shubhi, and his friend, Anjali. He had always been a responsible and mature person, but now he found himself struggling with a dilemma he could not resolve.

On the one hand, there was Shubhi, his best friend, who had been by his side through thick and thin. She was always there to support him and make him laugh, even in his most challenging moments. Shubhi's love confession caught him off guard, but he could not deny the special bond he shared with her.

On the other hand, there was Anjali, the girl he had fallen in love with. She was intelligent, funny, and had a great sense of humor. He loved her voice and how she talked and he felt a solid connection with her. Anjali's love confession had left him speechless, but he could not ignore his feelings for her.

Aadish was torn between his love for Anjali and his loyalty to Shubhi. He did not know what to do. Aadish knew that he could not hurt either of them, but at the same time, he did not want to lose either of them. He felt like he was walking on thin ice and was afraid of making the wrong decision.

He sought the advice of his closest friends, but he found that no one could give him the answers he was looking for. He was starting to feel overwhelmed and stressed and did not know how to handle the situation.

Aadish made a choice, but he soon realized it was not as easy as he thought it would be. The consequences of his decision would have far-reaching effects, and he would have to live with them for the rest of his life. He just hoped that he had made the right choice and that everything would work out for the best.

Over the next few days, Aadish spent much time reflecting on his feelings. He realized that he had developed deep feelings for Anjali, but he was scared of what would happen if things didn't work out. He knew he needed to be honest and tell her how he felt. Aadish thought about it and finally decided to be with Anjali. He strongly connected with her and believed they could build a future together.

However, little did Aadish know that this decision would have consequences that he couldn't have imagined. The confession of love by Anjali and Shubhi had changed their dynamic, and Aadish was now caught in two very different situations. He could only hope that everything would turn out well in the end.

So, he scheduled a video call with Anjali. During that call, he told her he had also fallen in love with her. They both were overjoyed, and their friendship transformed into a beautiful love story from that moment on.

CHAPTER THREE

Aadish and Anjali determined to meet. Anjali was a little nervous about finally meeting Aadish, but she was also excited. Anjali had counted the days until their meeting for weeks, and the day finally arrived. They agreed to meet in a park, and as soon as she saw him, Anjali knew she was in love.

The warm, golden rays of the sun gently kissed the skies as Anjali made her way to Lalbagh, a beautiful botanical garden in Indore. She was nervous, but at the same time, she felt an exhilarating rush of excitement as she anticipated seeing Aadish again. Anjali had been thinking about him constantly since he confessed his love for her.

As she walked through the lush green trees and the sweet aroma of flowers filled the air, Anjali spotted Aadish waiting for her by a large, flowering rose bush. He was dressed in a crisp white shirt and navy blue trousers, and Aadish styled his dark brown hair neatly. The sight of him took her breath away, and she couldn't help but smile as she approached him.

"Hello, Anjali," Aadish greeted her with a warm smile. "I'm so glad you came."

"I wouldn't have missed this for anything," Anjali replied, feeling butterflies in her stomach.

They strolled through the garden, admiring the different varieties of roses and the vibrant colors of the flowers.

They talked about their hopes and dreams for the future and laughed about memories from the past. They stopped at a serene pond and sat on a bench, taking in the peaceful surroundings.

As the sun began to dip below the horizon, Aadish reached into his pocket and pulled out a single, long-stemmed red rose. He handed it to Anjali, and she gasped in surprise.

"Aadish, it's beautiful," she said, admiring the rose's delicate petals and sweet fragrance.

"Just like you," Aadish said, his eyes shining with love.

At that moment, Anjali felt her heart swell with happiness. Despite all the uncertainty and difficulties she faced, she knew she wanted to be with Aadish forever.

As they walked back through the garden, hand in hand, Anjali made a decision. She would follow her heart and choose love, no matter the consequences. And with that, she felt a sense of peace and contentment, knowing that she had made the right choice.

CHAPTER FOUR

It had been two weeks since Anjali and Aadish had their first date at Lalbagh, and they had been inseparable ever since. Their love grew stronger daily, and they learned new things about each other. They would spend hours talking to each other on the phone, sharing their thoughts and feelings, and bonding over their similarities and differences.

One night, as they lay on their respective beds, talking on the phone, Anjali asked Aadish about his plans and aspirations. Aadish, feeling confident and open with her, shared that his lifelong dream was to become an author. He told her that he had always been passionate about writing and genuinely enjoyed it. However, Aadish also admitted that he always wanted one other thing in his future: to be with her. He expressed his feelings towards her and how she had been a significant source of inspiration for his writing. Anjali was touched by his words and felt a strong connection with him.

Anjali smiled at the other end of the phone, "I want to be a part of your future, Aadish. I want to support you in every way possible and help you achieve your dreams."

Aadish's heart swelled with love and gratitude. He had never felt this way before. He knew that he had found the love of his life in Anjali, and he was grateful for every moment they spent together.

As the night went on, they continued their conversation, talking about their hopes and fears, their families and friends, and the future they wanted to build together. They talked until the sun started to rise, and they had to hang up, promising each other to speak the next day again.

As they drifted to sleep, both Anjali and Aadish knew they were meant to be together. They had found their soulmates in each other, and nothing could ever come between them. They were confident that no matter what life threw their way, they would always find their way back to each other.

CHAPTER FIVE

It had been two weeks since Anjali and Aadish had their first date at Lalbagh, and they had been inseparable ever since. Their love grew stronger daily, and they learned new things about each other. They would spend hours talking to each other on the phone, sharing their thoughts and feelings, and bonding over their similarities and differences.

Anjali had never been much of a party person, but she was willing to go the extra mile for the man she loved. She talked to some of her close friends, and they were happy to help her with the arrangements. Anjali set the plan, and She fixed the date. It was to be a small intimate gathering of close friends and family, and the theme was a surprise.

The day finally arrived, and Anjali was a bundle of nerves. She had gone to great lengths to ensure everything was perfect and hoped that Aadish would love it. She decided to make a small speech on occasion and express her love for him.

As Aadish walked into the room, his loved ones greeted him with a loud chorus of 'Happy Birthday.' He was taken aback by sight in front of him. The room was decorated beautifully with balloons, streamers, and a birthday cake that looked like a work of art. He was surrounded by the people he loved the most, which was a surreal moment.

Anjali took the mic and started her speech. She talked about how much Aadish meant to her and how much she loved him. Anjali spoke of all the memories they had created together and how she couldn't wait to make many more. She ended her speech by saying she hoped this birthday would be the first of many more happy birthdays together.

Anjali was so nervous that she couldn't sleep. She had never felt this way before and was scared that something might go wrong. But as soon as she saw Aadish's smile the next day, all her fears vanished. The look of happiness and surprise on his face made all the effort worth it. Aadish was overjoyed by the shock and thanked Anjali for making his birthday special. He couldn't believe he had found such a caring and thoughtful person.

Aadish was overwhelmed by Anjali's words and her love for him. He hugged her tight and whispered in her ear, "I love you, Anjali, thank you for this surprise and for making my birthday so special. You are the best thing that has ever happened to me."

The birthday party continued with laughter, food, and lots of love. Aadish and Anjali spent the evening together, dancing and chatting with their loved ones. It was a night they would always cherish and a reminder of how much their love for each other had grown in just a short time.

As the night ended, Aadish and Anjali said their goodbyes and headed home. They lay in bed, entwined in each other's arms, and discussed the future. They talked about their dreams for themselves and each other and promised to support and stand by each other consistently.

The surprise birthday party had been an enormous success, and it was a testament to Anjali's love for Aadish. She had shown him that love can be expressed in so many ways and that she was willing to go the extra mile to make him happy. This was just the beginning of their love story, and they knew they had many more milestones to reach together.

CHAPTER SIX

The birthday of Aadish had come and gone, and his relationship with Anjali had grown more robust with each passing day. The couple had been spending more and more time together, and their love for each other grew stronger with each passing moment. However, this idyllic period was not meant to last.

Aadish finally started to feel like he was truly happy for the first time in a long time, and he thought Anjali felt the same way. But things began to change.

Aadish was going about his daily routine when he received a shocking call from his friend Kashravi. She informed him that she had seen Anjali in a cafe with her ex-boyfriend. Aadish was taken aback and couldn't believe what he was hearing. Kashravi tried to reassure him, explaining that she wasn't sure what was going on, but she had thought it was important to let him know. Aadish was grateful for her honesty, but he couldn't shake the feeling of hurt that had settled in the pit of his stomach. He wasn't sure how to process the information or how to confront Anjali about it. The news hit Aadish like a ton of bricks, as he had always trusted Anjali and believed their relationship was rock solid. He felt a rush of emotions as he tried to process the information, feeling hurt and confused about what was happening. He was torn between wanting to confront Anjali and giving her the benefit of the doubt.

Despite his reservations, he confronted Anjali about the situation, hoping to get some answers and clarity about what was happening in their relationship.

The fight was about something that Aadish had discovered. He had found out that Anjali had secretly visited her ex-boyfriend, despite being in a committed relationship with him. Aadish was hurt and confused. He couldn't understand why Anjali would do something like this behind his back. He confronted her about it, but Anjali refused to give him a straight answer. Instead, she became defensive and started to argue with him.

Aadish had just finished his call with Anjali and felt mixed emotions. He was feeling confused, angry, and hurt. Aadish had no idea why Anjali acted like this; he thought they had a strong connection and were building a future together. He tried to make sense of the situation but couldn't find any answers.

Days went by, and Anjali didn't return his calls or messages. Aadish tried to reach out to her, but all he got were excuses. She was busy with work, out of town, her phone was broken, and so on. Aadish started to doubt if their relationship was real or just a fleeting moment of passion. He wanted to believe in their love, but the lack of communication and excuses made it more complicated.

Shubhi noticed something was off with Aadish and asked him what was happening. When he told her about the situation with Anjali, she listened attentively and tried to offer some comfort. She told him that Anjali was probably going through some tough times and needed space, but she also warned him not to let himself be mistreated.

Aadish appreciated Shubhi's advice, but he couldn't shake off the feeling that there was more to the story. He decided to take time to clear his mind and refocus on his life. He threw himself into his work and tried to keep himself busy, but the thoughts of Anjali lingered in his mind.

As the days passed, Aadish realized that he couldn't keep making excuses for Anjali's behavior. He needed to talk with her and find out what was happening. He hoped their love was strong enough to weather any storm, but he couldn't ignore the fact that things were changing. He needed to know if their relationship was worth fighting for or if it was time to let it go.

Aadish was left feeling frustrated and confused. He tried to shake it off, telling himself that she was probably having a bad day, but he couldn't help feeling worried. Was she losing interest in their relationship? Was she pulling away from him? He didn't know what was happening, but he knew he wanted to find out.

He spent the next few days in a state of tension, constantly checking his phone for messages from Anjali and trying to keep busy to take his mind off things. He felt like he was walking on eggshells, not knowing what to expect from her anymore. He couldn't help feeling irritable and on edge and snapping at his friends and family over minor things.

CHAPTER SEVEN

Anjali's heart was pounding as she picked up the phone. It was Shubhi, and Anjali was unsure if she was ready to face his best friend after everything that had happened.

Hey, Shubhi," she answered, trying to keep her voice steady.

Shubhi didn't waste any time getting straight to the point.

Anjali, what's going on with you and Aadish?

He's been a mess ever since your birthday. He's not eating; he's not sleeping; he's just been moping around like a lost soul.

Anjali's heart ached as she listened to Shubhi's words. She knew that she had hurt Aadish deeply by visiting to her ex, but she felt like she had no other choice at the time.

"I'm sorry, Shubhi," she whispered.

"I just... I didn't know what to do."

"Well, you need to do something now," Shubhi said firmly.

Aadish is my best friend, and I can't stand to see him like this. He loves you, Anjali. And I know that you love him too. You need to make a choice, and you need to make it soon. Because if you don't, you'll lose him forever.

Anjali hung up the phone, her heart heavy with regret. She knew that Shubhi was right. Anjali needed to make a choice, and she needed to make it soon. She didn't know if she was ready to face the consequences of her heart's choice.

She sat there in silence, her thoughts swirling until the phone rang again.

This time, it was Aadish. "Anjali?" he said, his voice barely above a whisper. "Can we talk?"

Anjali took a deep breath, steeling herself for what was to come.

"Yes," she said. "We need to talk." And with that, she braced for the most complicated conversation of her life.

CHAPTER EIGHT

One day, Anjali went to visit her ex-boyfriend, and this caused a great deal of tension between her and Aadish. Anjali had never been completely honest with Aadish about her past relationship and why it had ended. Aadish, who was very close to Anjali, was deeply hurt by this revelation and felt betrayed. He thought Anjali had not been completely honest with him, causing a rift in their relationship.

Shubhi, Aadish's best friend, noticed something was amiss and decided to intervene. She sat down with Aadish and listened as he shared his feelings about Anjali's visit to her ex-boyfriend. Shubhi understood why Aadish was feeling hurt and tried to comfort him. She explained that everyone makes mistakes and that Anjali still loved him deeply.

Despite Shubhi's best efforts, the tension between Anjali and Aadish continued to grow. They stopped spending as much time together, and their conversations became strained and tense. The love they once shared seemed to be slipping away, and both were feeling the weight of this growing tension.

Anjali, who was deeply ashamed of her actions, tried to make amends with Aadish. She apologized for not being completely honest with him and promised to be more open. However, Aadish's hurt was too deep, and he could not forgive her completely.

The tension between Anjali and Aadish continued to build, and it seemed as though their relationship was on the brink of collapse. With each passing day, the love they once shared became a distant memory. Will their love survive this turmoil, or will it be lost forever?

CHAPTER NINE

The following day, Aadish woke up with a sense of unease. Had seemed distant on the phone the previous night. He couldn't shake the feeling that something was wrong. He tried to call her, but her phone went straight to voicemail.

As Aadish prepared for his upcoming basketball match, his thoughts were consumed by the tension building up inside of him. Anjali's recent behavior had bothered him, and he couldn't help but feel like something was off. Despite his best efforts to push these thoughts aside, they lingered in the back of his mind, weighing heavily on him. To make matters worse, he was also stressed about the upcoming match - it was crucial for his team, and a victory would mean a chance at the nationals. The pressure to perform was immense, and Aadish felt the weight of it all. He was running through plays, practicing his shots, and trying to focus, but his thoughts kept drifting back to Anjali. He couldn't shake the feeling that something was wrong and affecting his game. With each passing day, the tension grew, and Aadish felt like he was about to snap.

Aadish was in the middle of his training session when his phone rang. It was Anjali.

He quickly wiped the sweat from his forehead and answered the call, "Hey Anjali."

But instead of the cheerful tone he was used to hearing, Anjali's voice was heavy with tears.

"Aadish, I'm sorry. I need to talk to you."

Aadish's heart started racing. He could sense that something was wrong.

He decided to visit her and try to get to the bottom of things. When he arrived at her apartment, he found her sitting on the couch, looking troubled.

"Anjali, what's going on?" he asked, sitting beside her.

"Aadish, I have something to tell you," she said, looking at him with tears. "I've been seeing my ex again and realized that I still have feelings for him."

Aadish felt as though he had been punched in the gut, and He had never expected this.

"I'm sorry, Aadish," Anjali continued. "I never meant to hurt you. But I must follow my heart, telling me to be with him."

Aadish didn't know what to say. He felt like his world was falling apart. He had never been in love before, and now he was losing the only person he had ever loved.

He stood up and walked to the door, his heart heavy with the knowledge that this was the end. He turned to Anjali and looked into her eyes.

"I hope you'll be happy with him," he said and then walked out the door, not knowing what the future would hold for him.

As he walked down the street, he thought about the consequences of a heart's choice. He follows his heart and falls in love with Anjali, but in the end, it leads to heartbreak. He realized that sometimes, the heart's choice may not always lead to happiness, but it was a risk he was willing to take, no matter the outcome.

CHAPTER TEN

Aadish felt as if his heart had been ripped out of his chest. He had never imagined that Anjali would choose her ex over him. Despite knowing the truth, he couldn't shake the feeling of love he had for her. He tried to distract himself by immersing himself in work, but nothing seemed to take away the pain.

Days turned into weeks and weeks into months, but the pain only seemed to intensify for Aadish. He was struggling to cope with the loss he had experienced. Shubhi tried to be there for him, offering him comfort and support, but despite her best efforts, he couldn't help but push her away. He felt like a shell of his former self and didn't know how to move on.Shubhi, on the other hand, was heartbroken to see the person she loved so much in such a state of despair. She felt helpless and didn't know what to do to help him.

One day, he found himself roaming the city, lost in thought. He remembered the memories he had shared with Anjali and their love. He felt he would never be able to love again and was destined to be alone.

As he walked, he found himself at the edge of Lalbagh, the same place where he had taken Anjali on their first date. The memories came flooding back, and he broke down in tears. At that moment, he realized he needed to accept the truth and move on with his life. He couldn't hold onto the past forever and needed to find a way to heal and begin anew.

He slowly started to rebuild his life with Shubhi by his side. He began to see the beauty in life again and found solace in his work. He was finally starting to heal and was ready to face the future with hope and determination.

But, Aadish was devastated after Anjali chose her ex over him. He felt like his world had come crashing down, and all his hopes and dreams had been shattered. He struggled to get through each day, constantly feeling heavy on his heart. His best friend Shubhi, however, was there for him every step of the way.

Despite her busy schedule, Shubhi made it a point to spend time with Aadish, whether just hanging out, watching a movie, or going for a walk. She listened to him when he needed to vent his frustrations and offered encouragement and comfort when he felt down. She was always there to pick him up when he was feeling low.

Shubhi was there for him every step of the way. She listened to him when he needed someone to talk to and provided a shoulder to cry on when he needed it. She encouraged him to focus on himself and to start the healing process.

One day, as they were sitting on the couch together, Shubhi turned to Aadish and said, "You know, I've always been here for you, and I always will be. I care about you, and I want to see you happy. I know this is difficult for you, but I believe you'll come out of this stronger and happier in the end."

Aadish couldn't help but feel grateful for Shubhi's unwavering support. She was his rock, and he knew he could always count on her. With her by his side, he felt like he could face anything, and he started to see a glimmer of hope on the horizon.

Aadish started to take small steps towards moving on. He threw himself into work, took up a new hobby, and made an effort to spend time with his friends. Slowly but surely, he started to feel better.

However, he still couldn't shake the thoughts of Anjali. He constantly wondered if she was happy with her ex and if she was regretting her decision to end things with him.

Shubhi suggested they go out and do something fun together. She wanted to take his mind off Anjali and help him move on once and for all. Aadish agreed, and they went on a road trip together.

The fresh air and change of scenery did wonders for Aadish. He finally started to feel like himself again. He was grateful to have Shubhi by his side, supporting him through this difficult time.

As they continued their journey, Aadish realized that he had started forming feelings for Shubhi. She was kind and caring and had always been there for him. He was beginning to see her in a new light and was excited about what the future might hold for them.

Aadish's journey to move on was long and challenging, but with the support of Shubhi, he was finally able to find happiness once again. He was ready to start a new chapter with a new love and perspective.

Aadish realized that he was truly blessed to have Shubhi in his life. Her unwavering support and friendship played a huge role in helping him overcome his difficult times. Through their conversations, he learned that Shubhi had been going through her own struggles, and they could support each other in ways only true friends could. Over time, their bond grew stronger, and their love for each other evolved into something more. It wasn't until this point that Aadish truly understood the power of friendship and its role in our lives. He was grateful for every moment they spent together and cherished the memories they had created. Despite the ups and downs of life, he knew that Shubhi would always be there for him and for her, and he was thankful for their beautiful friendship.

And so, as Aadish continued to move forward and find happiness again, he knew that Shubhi would always be there, cheering and supporting him through thick and thin.

CHAPTER ELEVEN

Anjali was in turmoil as she struggled with her decision to be with her ex instead of Aadish. Despite the promises made to her by her ex, Anjali couldn't ignore the emptiness she felt in her heart. She missed the moments she shared with Aadish and their laughter. Their memories consumed her thoughts, and she felt a strong pull to be with him. Every day, her thoughts returned to Aadish, and she couldn't help but wish she was still by his side. She felt a deep longing for the love and happiness only Aadish could bring her life. Anjali was torn between her present reality and her enthusiasm for her past with Aadish.

Anjali was going through a whirlwind of emotions as she realized her true feelings for Aadish. Despite being in a relationship with someone else, her heart was drawn to Aadish, and her love for him was as strong as ever. The thought of losing him forever was like a knife twisting in her heart, and she couldn't help but feel regret for her past decisions. The realization of her love for Aadish was overwhelming, and she felt a sense of longing for him that was impossible to ignore. She couldn't stop thinking about him, and the memories of their time together were constantly replaying in her mind. Anjali was struggling with her emotions, and she knew she needed to make a decision that would determine her future. Would she stay with the person she was with, or would she follow her heart and be with Aadish? The thought of it was daunting, but deep down, she knew what she truly wanted.

Anjali's mind was consumed with thoughts of Aadish and the love they once shared. She had fallen hard for him, and his attention and affection had made her feel like she was on top of the world. The way he had looked at her with love in his eyes was something she would never forget, and how his touch had made her feel still lingered in her heart. She missed the sound of his voice and how he had made her feel special, and she couldn't help but question if she would ever experience that kind of love again. The passing days only seemed to heighten the emptiness she felt without him. Anjali knew she had to face her feelings and the possibility that she may never be able to be with Aadish again, but it was a daunting and painful thought.

She realized her mistake in choosing her ex-boyfriend over Aadish. She knew that her actions had caused immense pain to Aadish, and the thought of losing him forever was devastating. The realization that her selfishness led to hurting the person she truly loved overwhelmed her and filled her with regret and sadness. Anjali knew she had to make things right and try to mend her relationship with Aadish. She was determined to show him she was genuinely sorry for her actions and prove their love was worth fighting for.

Despite her struggles, Anjali remained hopeful that she could make things right with Aadish and win back his love. She knew it wouldn't be easy, but she was willing to do whatever it took to make things right and have a future filled with love and happiness.

CHAPTER TWELVE

Anjali couldn't help but think about all the moments they shared, from their first date to their last argument. She remembered how he used to make her laugh and always knew how to cheer her up when she was feeling down. But as she kept scrolling through their memories, the reality of their breakup hit her like a ton of bricks. Tears filled her eyes as she realized she had lost the person she thought she would spend the rest of her life with. The thought of never being able to have those moments again was unbearable, and she couldn't help but feel like she was the one who had pushed him away. She took a deep breath and tried to shake the feelings of regret and sadness. She knew that dwelling on the past wouldn't change anything, but it was hard to move on when her heart was still broken.

Anjali remembered the day she opened up to Aadish about her past relationship and her decision-making process. The pain and sadness in Aadish's eyes still haunted her. She had been selfish, only thinking about her own emotions and not considering their impact on Aadish. As he walked away, his hurt expression burned into her memory. Despite loving him deeply, she had caused him immense pain, and she regretted it deeply. She realized that true love meant putting the other person's feelings and well-being above her own, and she had failed.

Anjali realized she had made a huge mistake and wanted another chance with Aadish. She picked up her phone and dialed his number, her heart racing as she waited for him to answer.

"Hello?" Aadish answered, his voice cold and distant.

"Aadish, it's Anjali. I just wanted to talk to you and tell you how sorry I am for everything. I never meant to hurt you, and I realize now that I made a mistake in choosing my ex over you," she said, her voice shaking.

"Anjali, I appreciate the apology, but it's too little too late," Aadish replied his voice firm. "I've moved on, and I don't think it's a good idea for us to talk. I wish you all the best, but I must let go of the past."

Anjali felt her heart break as she listened to Aadish's words. She had lost him, and there was no going back. She hung up the phone, tears streaming down her face as she realized that the love of her life was gone forever.

This was the heart-wrenching truth that Anjali had to face. She had let go of the love she had found with Aadish, and now, she was left with nothing but her regrets. She knew that moving forward would be a long and challenging journey, but she was determined to learn from her mistakes and become a better person.

As Anjali sat reflecting on her past experiences with love, she was filled with mixed emotions. She realized that love was a rare and valuable treasure that should be cherished and appreciated. She had learned so much about herself and her relationships through her journey and was grateful for the lessons she had gained. Despite the loss of the love of her life, Anjali knew that she could not dwell on the past and had to move forward. She took a moment to gather herself and take a deep breath, ready to embark on a new chapter of her life with a newfound appreciation for the power of love. She was determined to keep the memories of her past close to her heart and to continue growing and learning as she navigated her future.

CHAPTER THIRTEEN

As the days passed, Aadish and Anjali found themselves constantly thinking about each other. Although they had both moved on with their lives, they couldn't deny the intense connection they still felt. The memories of their time together were like a warm glow in their hearts, reminding them of the happiness they had shared. Despite the challenges they had faced and the mistakes, they had made, their love for each other remained strong. They both longed to be together again, to hold each other and pick up where they left off they didn't know if they would ever be able to make that happen. As they went about their daily lives, they couldn't help but wonder if they would ever be able to be together again and start a new chapter in their lives.

It was a warm summer day when Aadish received an invitation to a reunion party organized by some mutual friends. At first, he was hesitant to attend, knowing that Anjali would also be there. But with some encouragement from Shubhi, his best friend, he decided to go and face his past.

Aadish went to the reunion; as soon as he walked into the room, his eyes locked onto Anjali's. It was as if time had stood still for a moment and all the pain and heartache that had once separated them faded. They shared a warm smile but kept a safe distance, knowing they were not ready to rekindle their romance.

They chatted and caught up with old friends throughout the evening, secretly wishing they could be alone together. But as the night drew to a close and the partygoers began to disperse, they found themselves standing face to face, unsure what to say or do.

"I'm sorry," Anjali said, her voice soft and filled with regret.

"I know I hurt you, and I'm so sorry for that."

Aadish nodded, his eyes welling up with tears. "I've had time to heal and move on, but that doesn't mean the pain has completely gone away," he said. "I'm glad we can at least be friends again."

And with that, they hugged each other tightly, feeling a sense of closure and hope for the future. Although they would always love each other, they knew their paths led them differently.

As the night ended, Aadish and Anjali parted ways, feeling a sense of peace and closure. They had finally come to terms with their relationship and were ready to move forward with their lives. Although their love story ended, it still held a special place in their hearts. It was a reminder of the memories they had shared and the lessons they had learned. They were grateful for their time together and their love, but they also knew it was time to let go and start a new chapter. They said their goodbyes, promising to always cherish the memories they had made, and went their separate ways, knowing that their paths would cross again someday.

CHAPTER FOURTEEN

The reunion between Aadish and Anjali was a turning point in their lives. After that fateful day, they both knew they were not meant to be together. Aadish was heartbroken, but he tried to put on a brave face for the sake of his friends and family. He threw himself into his studies, determined to do well in the upcoming JEE exams.

He realized that his future was in his hands and that he needed to put in all his effort to crack JEE. He started studying for longer hours and cutting down on his social life, determined to give his all to his exams. He felt that it was the best way to move forward after the heartbreak and prove to himself that he could achieve his dreams, regardless of what happened in his personal life.

Aadish was in a tough spot. He had been going through a difficult breakup with Anjali and was now focusing all his energy on preparing for the Joint Entrance Exam (JEE). The pressure was mounting, and the exams were fast approaching. Aadish had always been a determined and hardworking individual, but now that he was single and had a clear head, he was more driven than ever to succeed. He had a strong desire to prove to himself and those around him that he could achieve his dreams and that he would not let anything stand in his way. He was focused and disciplined and worked day and night tirelessly, pouring over his textbooks and practicing problems until his mind was exhausted. Despite the stress and tension, he remained resolute and refused to be swayed by distractions. He was determined to come out on top and show that he was a winner, both in love and life.

Now, Aadish's life was at a crossroads. He had just cleared the Joint Entrance Exam (JEE) but had yet to get admission into IIT. But this was not the end for Aadish. He had another option, to pursue his bachelor's degree in Bristol. It was a new journey, a new chapter in his life, but he was unsure about it.

He had worked hard for this opportunity, and it felt like all his efforts had gone to waste. Despite this setback, he tried to stay positive and was grateful that he had received an offer to study at Bristol University.

Bristol was a completely new environment, away from the familiar surroundings of Indore and his best friend, Shubhi. She had always been a support system for Aadish, giving him the motivation he needed. But now, he was going to be away from her, in a new city, and with new people. The thought of being far from his best friend was scary, bringing uncertainty to Aadish's mind.

However, despite all these thoughts, Aadish knew that he had to take the leap of faith. He packed his bags and left for Bristol. As Aadish walked towards the boarding gate at the airport, his mind was filled with mixed emotions. He was excited to start a new chapter in his life by studying in Bristol, but the thought of leaving behind his past, especially Anjali, was bothering him. Despite their breakup, the memories of their relationship still lingered in his mind, and he couldn't help but feel a wave of pain as he thought about their fights and the moments of happiness they shared. The argument still haunted him when he discovered that Anjali had visited her ex-boyfriend behind his back. He felt betrayed and heartbroken at that moment, and it still affected him. He tried to push these thoughts aside as he got in line to board the flight, but they kept coming back.

Nevertheless, he managed to board the flight, determined to start afresh and move forward with his life. The journey was long, and he had to face many challenges. There were moments when he felt homesick and missed his friends and family. But, he kept himself motivated by his goal, his dream of pursuing his education.

Aadish finally landed in Bristol after a long and tiring flight. He felt a sense of relief as he stepped out of the airport and took in the new surroundings. Despite his excitement to start a new chapter in his life, he couldn't shake off the memories of his past with Anjali. However, he was determined to put the past behind him and move forward. He went straight to his apartment, provided by the university, and settled in. The next day, he visited the migration office at Bristol University to complete all the necessary legal procedures and get all the information he needed to start his life in Bristol. He roamed the city and explored its beauty, trying to get a feel for his new home. He was determined to make the most of his fresh start and forget about the past.

The next day, Aadish stepped into the university campus, feeling nervous and overwhelmed. It was his first day of college, and he was surrounded by unfamiliar faces. Despite his best efforts, he couldn't shake off the feeling of hesitation as he approached the building. He was still coming to terms with the fact that he was thousands of miles away from home, starting a new life in a foreign land. Just as he was about to enter the classroom, a group of Indian students approached him. They introduced themselves as Gargi, Arush, and Zahra and welcomed him to Bristol University. Aadish felt an immediate sense of comfort and relief. It was good to know that other students from India were going through the same thing as him. As they chatted, he realized they were all studying the same course and would be classmates. The nervousness slowly faded, and Aadish felt a glimmer of hope that he could make it through this new chapter of his life.

In Bristol, Aadish started his new life. He made new friends, and the place was slowly starting to feel like home. But he still missed Shubhi.

Aadish was adapting to his new life, but he was still unsure about the future. He had a new chapter in his life, but it was uncertain and full of challenges. However, he was determined to face them head-on and make the most of his journey in Bristol.

CHAPTER FIFTEEN

Aadish had been in Bristol for several months, enjoying his life there. He studied hard, made new friends, and adapted to the new culture. Despite all of this, he still missed his best friend, Shubhi. They used to be inseparable back in India, but now they were oceans apart. He longed to hear her voice and see her smile. The distance had made him realize the depth of his feelings for her.

Aadish and Shubhi struggled to maintain their bond as their physical distance had increased significantly. With Aadish in Bristol and Shubhi in India, the time difference made it difficult for them to communicate. They could only exchange text messages, which left them feeling like they had lost the closeness they once shared. Despite the difficulties, they tried to stay in touch, but the conversations lacked the depth they once had. The daily phone calls and texts were a constant reminder of the physical distance between them, and the feelings of sadness and longing grew stronger with each passing day. The once tight-knit friendship now seemed to be drifting apart, and they both wondered if they would ever be able to regain the bond they once shared.

Shubhi missed Aadish terribly, and the distance between them made her miss him more. She constantly worried about her best friend. She remembered all the memories they made together and how much they relied on each other for comfort and support. She felt insecure about the fact that they were so far from each other and could only communicate through texts and calls. She feared that their bond would weaken with time and distance and that they would drift apart. Shubhi, the protective and concerned friend she was, constantly tried to reach out to Aadish and check on him. She sent him messages asking about his well-being and his life in Bristol. She wanted to ensure that he was happy and comfortable in his new surroundings and that their friendship remained intact despite the distance.

She wanted to be there for him and ensure their friendship remained strong. This led her to make the spontaneous decision to visit Aadish in Bristol. She applied for a visa and finally received it after a month of waiting. However, she kept the news to herself and didn't tell Aadish she was coming to see him. Shubhi had her end-semester exams approaching, but she felt she couldn't wait any longer to see her best friend. She took the bet and booked her tickets without telling Aadish. She was eager and excited to finally see Aadish after such a long time, even if it was just for a day.

Shubhi's excitement peaked as she boarded the flight to Bristol. Her thoughts were filled with the anticipation of finally seeing her best friend, Aadish, after such a long time. She reminisced about their childhood memories and all the fun times they had spent together. The thought of finally being able to hug him and catch up on everything brought a smile to her face. The long flight seemed like a breeze as she went through the pictures and videos of them together, reliving their moments. She was longing and eager to reach her destination as soon as possible. Even though her visit was going to be short, just a day, she was grateful for this opportunity to spend some quality time with Aadish. She couldn't wait to land in Bristol.

Shubhi had finally landed in Bristol after a long journey, and just after landing, she sent a text to Aadish that she had fallen down the stairs and had gotten stitches. Aadish was sitting in his study room, surrounded by books and notes. His focus was entirely on his upcoming exams. He quickly opened it to read, "Aadish, I fell down the stairs and I need your help. Please call me." Aadish's heart dropped at the thought of Shubhi being hurt. He immediately Facetimed her, but as soon as he saw her face on the screen, he was in for a surprise. Instead of seeing the hospital behind her, he saw the Bristol airport and realized he had been pranked. Despite the joke, he was overjoyed to see Shubhi, and he quickly told her to wait for him as he was picking her up.

Shubhi could see Aadish's car pull up at the airport, and as she stepped out of the terminal, she was overcome with emotion at the sight of her best friend. When Aadish finally reached her, he looked at her with a mixture of concern and happiness and asked her in a voice filled with emotion, "What are you doing here? I can't believe you're here!"

"I needed to see you," she said, her eyes filling with tears. "I've missed you so much. You are my best friend, and I just couldn't bear the thought of being apart from you any longer."

Aadish felt a sense of guilt as he realized that he had been so focused on his own life that he had neglected his best friend. He had taken her for granted, and now she was here, telling him how much she missed him.

"I'm sorry, Shubhi," he said, feeling ashamed. "I should have kept in touch with you. I just got so caught up in my own life."

Shubhi smiled at him, forgiving him instantly. "It's okay," she said. "I understand. And I'm here now, so let's make the most of our time together."

They went around the city, visiting various landmarks and taking in the sights and sounds of Bristol. As they walked, Shubhi told Aadish about everything happening in India and how much she missed him. She said it was not the same without him, and everyone was asking about him. Aadish felt a pang of sadness in his heart, realizing how much he had left behind.

Shubhi then took him to a small, quaint café and ordered their favourite drinks. They sat down and chatted for hours, reliving old memories and discussing their plans. Shubhi was excited to hear about Aadish's life in Bristol and how he was adjusting to the new city and culture.

Shubhi was in Bristol for just a day, but she was able to meet some of Aadish's new friends. Gargi, Arush, and Zahra were all students from India who were studying at Bristol University with Aadish. They were all friendly and welcoming to Shubhi, and she was glad to have met them. As she spent time with the group, she could see how close they had all become in such a short period. Despite being away from home, Aadish had found a new community of friends with whom he shared a strong bond. Shubhi was happy for her best friend, and she was grateful for the opportunity to meet his new friends and get a glimpse into his life in Bristol. She couldn't help but feel a little envious of the tight-knit group, but she was also happy that Aadish was doing well and enjoying his time in Bristol.

The day ended, Aadish and Shubhi faced the harsh reality that their time together was ending. Aadish was filled with emotion as he looked at Shubhi and realized how much he would miss her. He felt an emptiness as he thought about her leaving and returning to India. Shubhi, too, was feeling emotional. She had come all this way to see Aadish, and now their time was up. The thought of leaving him made her heart ache. They hugged each other tightly, holding on to each other, not wanting to let go. Tears rolled down their cheeks as they said their goodbyes. It was a bittersweet moment, filled with both happiness and sadness. As Shubhi boarded her flight back to India, Aadish felt a deep sense of loss. He had never felt this way before and didn't know how to deal with it. He stood at the airport, watching the plane take off into the sky, feeling a part of himself leave with it.

As he settled back into his routine in Bristol, Aadish couldn't help but think about the unexpected visit from Shubhi and how much it had brightened his day. He made a mental note to call her more often and to stay in touch with his friends back home. No matter where life took him, he knew that his roots and friends would always be a part of him.

CHAPTER SIXTEEN

Gargi, Arush, and Zahra were intrigued by Shubhi as soon as they met her. They could sense the special bond between her and Aadish, and they started teasing him about her being his girlfriend. They were amazed that he had never told them about her. The whole group was in fits of laughter as they joked about how cute the two looked together and how they made a perfect pair. Despite Aadish's initial embarrassment, he couldn't help but smile at their lighthearted teasing. The group's playful banter only confirmed what he already knew deep down in his heart – that he and Shubhi were meant to be together.

Aadish's feelings for Shubhi became clearer after she visited Bristol. Although he tried to ignore these feelings, his friends Gargi, Arush, and Zahra quickly pointed them out. They teased him with the idea that Shubhi was his girlfriend and that they made a cute couple. Despite their teasing, Aadish was still confused about his feelings and avoided discussing them. However, the thought of Shubhi traveling from India to visit him in Bristol made him question his feelings even more. He couldn't deny the fact that there was a strong connection between them, and the idea of them being together seemed perfect to his friends. Despite his confusion, Aadish couldn't ignore the feeling that there was something special between him and Shubhi, and he was starting to wonder if there was more to their friendship than he initially thought.

Aadish was in turmoil, trying to ignore his feelings for Shubhi, but they were constantly gnawing at him. Whenever he thought he had pushed them away, they returned with a vengeance. He tried to convince himself that it was just a passing infatuation, but deep down, he knew it was something more. He was afraid of what this meant, he had always seen Shubhi as just a friend, but now he realized his feelings for her were much more profound. He was confused and scared. He didn't know how to navigate this new territory. He constantly thought about Shubhi, imagining what it would be like to be with her. He knew he had to confront these feelings, but he wasn't sure how. He felt like he was in a constant state of limbo, unable to escape the thoughts and emotions that were swirling inside him.

Aadish had been struggling with his feelings for Shubhi for quite some time. He couldn't ignore how he felt about her anymore and knew he needed to talk to someone about it. He confided in his new friends Gargi, Arush, and Zahra. They were the only people he felt close to in Bristol, and he hoped they would understand. When he finally mustered up the courage to tell them about his feelings for Shubhi, they were supportive. They told him they could see how he lit up whenever Shubhi's name was mentioned and that he was in love with her. They convinced Aadish to embrace his feelings and tell Shubhi how he felt. They even offered to help him plan a surprise proposal for her. Aadish was hesitant initially, but with their encouragement, he decided to take the leap and finally confess his love to Shubhi.

Aadish was feeling nervous but determined to confess his feelings to Shubhi. He decided to do it on the upcoming Diwali vacation they would take in India. He believed

Diwali, the festival of lights would provide the perfect backdrop for his surprise proposal. Aadish confided in his friends Gargi, Arush, and Zahra about his plan, and they were happy to help him. They brainstormed and listed things they would need to make the proposal successful. Aadish's heart was racing with excitement and anticipation as he thought about finally expressing his love for Shubhi. He felt this would be the start of a new chapter in his life, and he couldn't wait to share it with the one he loved.

Aadish was determined to confess his feelings to Shubhi, so he planned a surprise proposal. He knew the upcoming Diwali vacation in India would be the perfect opportunity to pop the question. He also learned that Shubhi and her friends were going to watch a movie, so he took advantage of this opportunity. He coordinated with her friends and made arrangements to have a video he prepared to be played unexpectedly in the movie theater during the film. The footage would reveal his love for Shubhi and his intentions to propose to her. After the video ended, he would come out on stage and confess his feelings for her in front of everyone. Aadish was filled with nervous excitement as he carefully planned this particular moment, hoping that Shubhi would accept his proposal and start a new chapter in their lives together.

With the encouragement of his friends Gargi, Arush, and Zahra, he decided to create a surprise proposal video for her. With their help, he recorded a heartfelt message that revealed his love for Shubhi and how much she meant to him. He spoke about their shared memories and how he couldn't imagine his life without her. The video was a true expression of his feelings and showed how much effort he had put into making this moment special for Shubhi. The anticipation of her reaction filled him with excitement and nervousness, but he was confident that this was the right step for him to take. He couldn't wait for her to see the video and hopefully say yes to being with him forever.

CHAPTER SEVENTEEN

The day has finally arrived for Aadish to travel to India for Diwali and give his surprise proposal to Shubhi. He was filled with excitement and nervousness as he prepared for the trip. Aadish had been carefully planning this moment for weeks and had everything in place, from the video he would play in the movie hall to his heartfelt confession. He was determined to make this day special for Shubhi and was hopeful that she would feel the same way about him. Despite the butterflies in his stomach, Aadish was confident that this was the right decision, and he was eager to start his journey to India and make this Diwali one to remember.

As Aadish boarded the flight for India, his mind was filled with memories of the past, especially those with Shubhi. He thought about all the moments they shared, from their first meeting to their recent conversations. Despite being apart, their bond had only grown stronger, and Aadish couldn't help but feel grateful for Shubhi's presence in his life. Sitting in his seat, he went down memory lane and revisited their old conversations, laughter, and the silly moments they had shared. The thought of finally confessing his love for Shubhi filled Aadish with excitement and nervousness. He couldn't wait to see the look on her face when he proposed and hoped that she would feel the same way. As the flight took off,

Aadish closed his eyes and took a deep breath, mentally preparing himself for the biggest moment of his life.

Aadish was excited as he stepped off the plane in Indore, India. He couldn't wait to see his family and friends again, especially after being away in Bristol for so long. The familiar sights, sounds, and smells of India surrounded him as he made his way through the airport. He was eager to reunite with his parents, who he knew would be overjoyed to see him. He also looked forward to catching up with his old school friends, whom he hadn't seen in years. He felt a warm nostalgia wash over him as he thought about the good times they shared growing up in Indore. The excitement for the upcoming Diwali festival and his plan for the surprise proposal for Shubhi added an extra layer of anticipation to his visit. He couldn't wait to see everyone and start creating new memories in the place he used to call home.

Returning to his hometown and celebrating Diwali with his family, old friends, and school friends filled him with happiness. He greeted everyone warmly and was overjoyed to see everyone. Aadish felt that this Diwali would be the best yet, especially since he had a special surprise planned for Shubhi, his best friend. He visited everyone he could, including Shubhi's family, where he greeted everyone warmly, and Shubhi was overjoyed to see him. Despite the excitement and happiness, Aadish kept his surprise proposal for Shubhi a secret, not wanting to ruin the moment. He was excited as he thought about the next day, knowing it would be a day to remember.

It was the day of the surprise proposal, and Aadish felt nervous and excited. He had made all the arrangements and was waiting behind the stage in the cinema hall. Shubhi was coming with her friends to watch a movie, and Aadish was preparing to confess his love for her. The lights were dimmed, the film was about to start, and the stage was set for Aadish to make his grand entrance. He took a deep breath and prepared himself for the big moment. The excitement was palpable, and Aadish was filled with a mixture of nerves and joy as he thought about his love for Shubhi.

The movie was about to start, and Shubhi with her friends took their seats. Meanwhile, Aadish was behind the stage, constantly communicating with her friends to ensure everything went according to plan. The anticipation was palpable as Aadish waited for the right moment to make his grand appearance. He had worked so hard to plan this surprise proposal and wanted everything to be perfect. He had butterflies in his stomach as he thought about when he would finally confess his love to Shubhi. He took a deep breath, and then another, to calm his nerves and center himself before he went out there to take the stage. With every passing moment, he could feel his excitement growing, and he was more determined than ever to make this moment one that Shubhi would never forget.

As the lights dimmed and the movie started playing, it suddenly started crashing. And then, out of nowhere, the proposal video started playing on the big screen. Aadish's heart was pounding with anticipation. He had worked so hard to coordinate everything with Shubhi's friends, ensuring that the video would play at the right moment. As the proposal video started playing on the big screen, everyone in the cinema hall was cheering and clapping, but Shubhi was utterly bewildered. She had no idea what was happening and why a video featuring Aadish was playing in the middle of the movie. The video showed all the memories they had shared together and how much Aadish loved her. As the video ended, Aadish stepped out from behind the stage and got down on one knee. With tears in his eyes, he confessed his love for her and asked her to be his girlfriend. Everyone in the cinema hall was silent, waiting for Shubhi's response!

However, Shubhi's reaction was not what Aadish had expected. As she looked at him, she appeared confused and overwhelmed. She was taken aback by the sudden proposal and couldn't understand why Aadish would want to take their friendship to the next level. She thought about their past and how Aadish had chosen another girl, Anjali, over her. The memory of that hurt still lingered, and she wasn't sure if she was ready to take that risk again. Additionally, Shubhi valued their friendship profoundly and was not prepared to complicate things by adding a romantic element. She was torn between her feelings for Aadish and her desire to keep their friendship intact.

"Aadish, I can't do this," Shubhi said, her voice shaking.

"I love you, but I can't be with you like this.

I can't be in a relationship with you."

Aadish was heartbroken as he realized his feelings for Shubhi were not mutual. He had built up this elaborate plan to propose to her, only to discover that she did not feel the same way. He thought he had invested so much of himself into this relationship, but now it seemed like it was all for nothing. He couldn't believe that his hopes and dreams had been crushed so suddenly. He had always imagined a future with Shubhi by his side, but now that seemed like an impossible fantasy. He felt like he was in a daze, trying to come to terms with this new reality. Despite all the time and effort he had put into this relationship, it seemed like it was never meant to be. The thought of losing Shubhi was painful, and Aadish struggled to come to terms with it.

"I'm sorry, Aadish," Shubhi continued, tears streaming down her face. "I don't want to lose our bond, but I can't be with you romantically."

Aadish felt like he was in shock as he heard Shubhi say that she didn't feel the same way about him. All the plans and preparations for the surprise proposal seemed like a distant memory now. The thought of not being able to be with Shubhi, of losing her, was devastating for him. He had never felt so vulnerable and exposed before. He had always been confident in his feelings and his ability to express them, but now he was at a loss for words. He felt like he was losing a part of himself and didn't know how to cope with it. The cinema hall was suddenly too small, too confining, and he needed to get out, to escape the pain and the rejection. But he couldn't leave Shubhi there, not after all he had done to win her heart. He didn't know how to make things right between them, but he knew he had to try.

"I understand," Aadish said finally, his voice barely above a whisper. "I just wish things could have been different."

Shubhi hugged him, Aadish couldn't hold back his emotions any longer as he embraced Shubhi. He felt a rush of sadness as he thought about all the times he and Shubhi had spent together and how he had always believed they would end up together. But now, it seemed like that dream would never become a reality. Despite his best efforts, he couldn't shake the feeling that he had missed his chance to be with Shubhi, and he struggled to hide his disappointment. The proposal he had planned with so much care and attention now felt pointless, and he couldn't help but wonder if Shubhi felt the same way. The weight of his feelings was almost too much to bear, and he had to take a step back and try to collect himself. Despite all of this, he still loved Shubhi profoundly and hoped that, somehow, they could still find a way to make things work between them.

He had put all his hopes and dreams into that moment, and to have it all come crashing down was devastating. He felt like he had lost the love of his life and his best friend. The reality of the situation hit him hard, and he was consumed with sadness and disappointment. However, he was a strong person and knew he couldn't let this rejection define him. He looked at the situation differently and concluded that sometimes, no matter how much you love someone, it's just not meant to be. He knew that he needed to take some time to heal and move on from this experience. He promised to focus on his own growth and happiness and not let the rejection hold him back. Though it was a challenging journey, he was determined to come out stronger and find love in the future.

As his vacation was coming to an end, he decided to leave for Bristol to start afresh. However, the thoughts of what had happened still lingered in his mind. Despite his best efforts, he could not shake off the disappointment and sadness that had taken hold of him. When he arrived in Bristol, he tried to focus on his studies and move on with his life. He buried himself in his books and immersed himself in his coursework, hoping it would help him forget. Despite his best efforts, he found it hard to forget the past and the pain that came with it. As time passed, he and Shubhi lost contact, and he didn't hear from her again. Despite the distance, he couldn't help but wonder what had happened to her and what had caused them to drift apart.

Aadish was finally able to move on with his life and was fully immersed in his studies and social life in Bristol. He had made many new friends and was enjoying his newfound freedom. One day, as the New Year approached, his friends invited him to a party to celebrate the start of the year. Aadish agreed to attend, eager to let loose and have some fun after a long period of hard work and studying.

As New Year's Eve came and went, Aadish slowly settled back into his regular routine. With the end of the semester fast approaching, he was consumed by his studies and exams. Every day was spent buried in books and notes, his focus solely on acing his end-of-semester exams. This had become his new normal, and he pushed all thoughts of Shubhi and the heartbreak she had caused him to the back of his mind. The only thing that mattered now was his future and his education. The days flew by, each one filled with a rigorous study schedule, and before he knew it, his birthday had arrived.

It was a birthday like no other for Aadish. As he sat at his desk, surrounded by textbooks and notes, his phone lit up with a message from Shubhi. It read "Happy Birthday Homie!" in bold, cheerful letters. He couldn't help but smile as he read the words. It was exactly 12AM, and he was studying for his exams when he received the message.

The End?

About The Author

Hey Stranger,

I am Aadish Jain, the author of this book. I am thrilled to introduce my first literary work and share my thoughts, emotions, and experiences. Writing has always been a passion of mine, and this book has been a long-awaited dream come true.

I put my heart and soul into this story, bringing to life the characters, the struggles, and the triumphs. The journey was not easy, but the end result has been nothing short of fulfilling. This book will bring you joy, laughter, and maybe even a tear.

I want to express my gratitude to those who supported me throughout this process, especially my family and friends, who encouraged me to pursue my dream. Your unwavering faith in me has inspired me, and I cannot thank you enough.

I hope this book finds its way into your hearts and becomes a cherished memory. Thank you for allowing me to share my work with you.

You can know more about me on Instagram **@aadishhere**

Dear Readers,

I hope you enjoyed reading my book as much as I enjoyed writing it. If you would like to support my work, please leave a review for my book on Amazon and Flipkart or send me a direct message on Instagram **@aadishhere**. Your thoughts and opinions on my book will help me grow as a writer.

Thank you for your time and support!

Printed by Libri Plureos GmbH in Hamburg, Germany